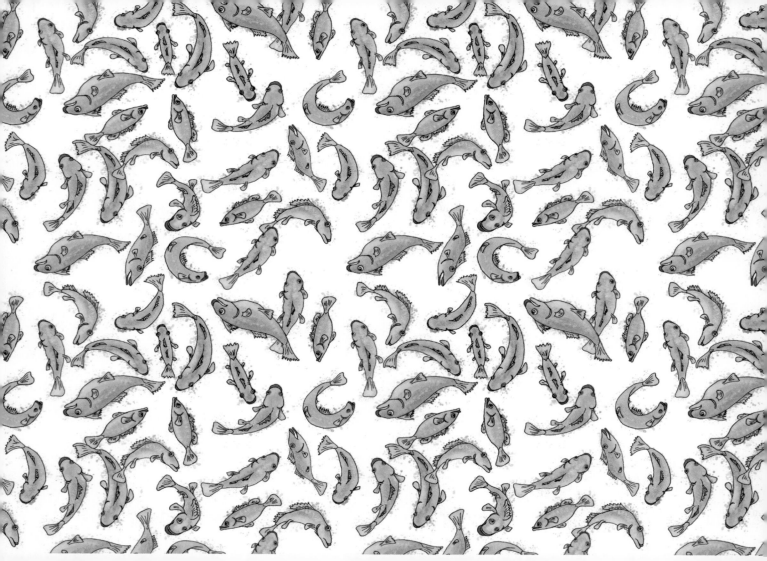

To Stephanie and Elaine, our long-suffering wives, for putting up with this nonsense for so many years, and a special mention to the alpacas in Katharine's doodle, spotted on Instagram, which sparked this alliance of authors and illustrator.

Introduction

The Authors

Spike

Tom

How the Camel and Wizard tale came to be

The year is 1979. The place is a vast, rambling old orphanage commandeered by the Civil Service to house the Department of Employment offices headquarters, which had become the daytime dwelling place for hundreds of pen-pushing civil servants.

Two of those civil servants are Spike Webb and Tom Graham, working in separate departments but in the same building. One morning, Spike, more bored than usual and disinclined to do any work, starts scribbling a few seemingly nonsensical verses of an improvised poem about a leaping camel, a wizard and some frying fish. He puts this into the internal post envelope and addresses it to Tom, who he assumes will be equally as bored and welcome an unexpected read.

On receipt of this a couple of hours later, Tom adds a few more verses to the poem and returns it, via the internal post messengers to Spike. This continues for a short while until both parties get bored of that too.

Ten years later both Spike and Tom leave the civil service to embark on different careers, but still keep in touch.

Many years later, Spike and Tom meet up for a drink and Tom mentions that over the years he has periodically revisited the 'camel' poem, adding verses to it. They decide that it's time to finish it, adding degrees of finesse, fine tuning and a fitting message to the reader.

So here it is, with its roots in a handful of rhyming couplets scribbled in a civil service office over forty years ago, re-visited from time-to-time over four decades and now beautifully illustrated by Katharine Harper, this extraordinary tale of moral dilemma has finally been completed.

The Camel and The Wizard

A journey from conflict to atonement

By Spike Webb and Tom Graham

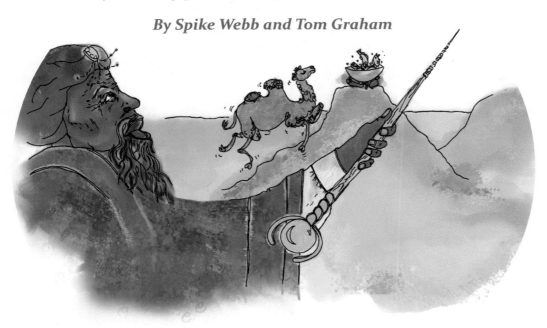

Illustrated by Katharine Harper

Part one

Conflict

People hear my story
it's no place for you or I
to writhe amongst the glory
of watching fishes fry!

Up and down the camel went
to watch the fishes fry,
but halfway down his fourth descent,
a wizard asked him why.

"Why do you jump and watch the fish?"
the purple wizard asked.
"It seems to me so cruel and ghoulish
to watch them breathe their last!"

But after this the wizard found
much to his dismay,
the camel was far below on the ground
and the answer he would not say.

"Oh come now please!" the wizard said
as the camel went on his course.
"They'll toss and turn until they're dead,
have you really no remorse?"

So halfway up he asked once more
"Why does this entertain?"
But before the camel could retort,
he was right at the top again.

"To tell the truth" the camel said
ascending by once more.
"If I want to see their fear and dread
it's no concern of yours!"

"I merely meant," the wizard said,
as the camel passed down below,
"one might have thought of tears to shed,
why mock their misery so?"

With every single leaping bound
the camel peeped in glee.
The purple wizard watched and frowned
and then did say to he...

"What is it about their desperate plight
that fills you with content?
And gives you such profane delight
during each obscene ascent?"

At this the camel had had too much,
"Enough", he cried "Enough!"
"It's not for you to be my judge"
then said quite loud and rough...

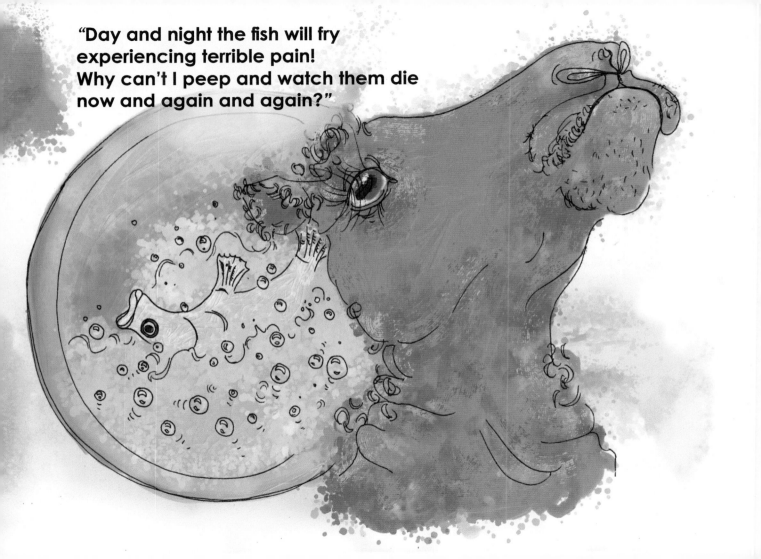

"Day and night the fish will fry
experiencing terrible pain!
Why can't I peep and watch them die
now and again and again?"

The wizard watched with sorrow deep
as some skewered fishes fried.
The camel peeped on every leap,
the wiz broke down and cried.

"Shame on you! Oh Shame on you!"
the wizard gribbed and grailed.
"A fish has feelings just like you,
why must they be impaled?"

The camel laughed while going up
and chuckled coming down.
"The juice of fish must fill my cup,"
he said, but with a frown.

"By Aaron's rod and Arthur's sword
I order you to cease!"

The wizard boomed
at such discord,
still the camel
watched his feast.

Through the night and through the day,
the camel spied his shoals.
The wizard on his knees would pray,
"God bless aquatic souls!"

"Oh Fishkind freedom!" begged the wiz
as the camel perused his fare.
Imperiled fish perceived as his
with not one shoal to share.

But up and down the camel jumped
and watched his fish with pride.
Never did a camel so humped,
enjoy a fish so fried!

The wizard full of anger shook,
dressed in purple from toe to head.
He gave the camel a hard stern look,
then this is what he said...

"Camel, you watch the fishes fry
and answer not my questions,
you're either down or up too high
but now you've tried my patience!"

The wizard drew his magic mace
and called the camel a sinner.
He then dislodged the dish of dace
that looked like Friday's dinner.

The camel cursed the wizard's ploy
and asked him while still crying,
"Why must you hinder me my boy
and upset my fishes frying!?"

The wizard who'd had enough of this,
pulled his wand from 'neath his hat.
He took his aim, vowed not to miss
and muttered some conjurer chat!

The wand it glowed so fiery hot,
it shook with sudden jolts,
and out a bolt of lightning shot
to the tune of 5000 volts!

It caught the camel by surprise
when he saw it in mid jump.
He screamed and tightly closed
both eyes,
then it hit him in the hump.

The camel's rump end hump exploded
with the force of a nuclear reaction!
Now the camel's DNA can be coded
as Dromedary rather than Bactrian!

The camel shrieked in anguish
as he landed from his jump.
For on the ground did languish
his charcoaled smoking hump.

"You'll pay for that," *the beast berated*
with full unbridled rage,
"The Gods will see you're castigated
you meddling purple sage!"

With that the heavens rumbled
and lightning lit the sky.
The wiz stepped back and stumbled
as the Gods appeared on high.

The Gods did cast a fiery glance,
the wizard bowed and cried,
"Should I have stayed away perchance
and left the fishes fried?"

A voice like roaring thunder
came from the sky above.
The wizard stood with wonder
eyes in his purple glove.

**"IF CAMEL WANTS TO
WATCH HIS FISH
AND IS PLEASURED AS
THEY FRY,
IT'S NOT FOR YOU TO
INTERFERE,
COMPLAIN OR VILIFY!"**

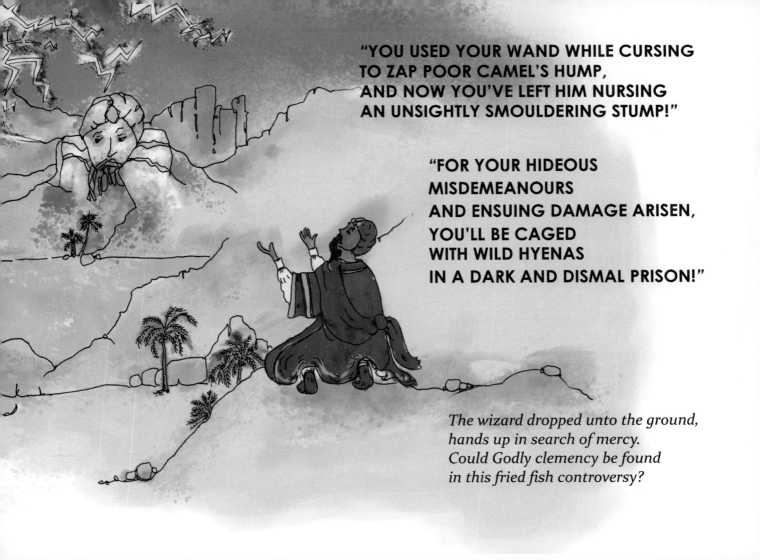

"YOU USED YOUR WAND WHILE CURSING
TO ZAP POOR CAMEL'S HUMP,
AND NOW YOU'VE LEFT HIM NURSING
AN UNSIGHTLY SMOULDERING STUMP!"

"FOR YOUR HIDEOUS
MISDEMEANOURS
AND ENSUING DAMAGE ARISEN,
YOU'LL BE CAGED
WITH WILD HYENAS
IN A DARK AND DISMAL PRISON!"

The wizard dropped unto the ground,
hands up in search of mercy.
Could Godly clemency be found
in this fried fish controversy?

"Please don't send me," the wizard uttered,
"To a secure institution."
'Neath his breath the camel muttered,
"How sweet this retribution!"

As the camel primed another jump,
The wiz sobbed, "I'm so sorry!
But just for the damage to your hump
not upsetting your fried fish quarry!"

"I'm sorry I destroyed your hump
where you store up all your water.
And now you'll need to use a pump,
'known better' I should have 'oughta'!"

"But I can't condone this obscene sham
of watching fishes fry.
Cod or bream or sprat or clam,
they don't deserve to die!"

The Camel stared at the purple sage
then cried to the Gods with reverence,
"Shall we cast him in the Hyena cage
or show him some benevolence?"

The Gods all whispered in a huddle
and discussed the nitty gritty
of this feisty fishy frying muddle,
then agreed to show some pity.

"You will not be cast in heavy chains!"
the wisely Gods admonished,
"But for inflicting Camel's rear
hump pains
from this land you will be banished!"

"Leave this land of frying fishes,
forget your fishy frying fears,
and stay exiled against you wishes,
for four and twenty years!"

As the wizard was escorted
by the Gods appointed guard,
to the border and deported
he cried out loud and hard....

"I swear by the sacred
Warlock oath
that I will complete my mission.
To save poor briny mites I quoth,
and steer this frying to remission"

"So Listen up and listen good
and camel hear my vow,
I **WILL** return to where I'm stood,
two dozen years from now!"

The camel stood and watched until
the wizard disappeared,
up and over the brow of the hill...

then the camel slowly sneered:

"Day and night my fish will fry
experiencing terrible pain.
I **WILL** peep and watch them die,
now and again and again!"

With that the camel turned around
and walked back to his rocky ledge,
that bore witness on that fishy mound
to the heinous crimes alleged.

So up and down the camel jumped
to watch his fishes fry.
The camel with his back so humped
and evil in his eye.

And there was no wiz, no purple sage
to upset his fishes fry.
No mauvish, mulberry magus rage...
no-one to ask him...Why?

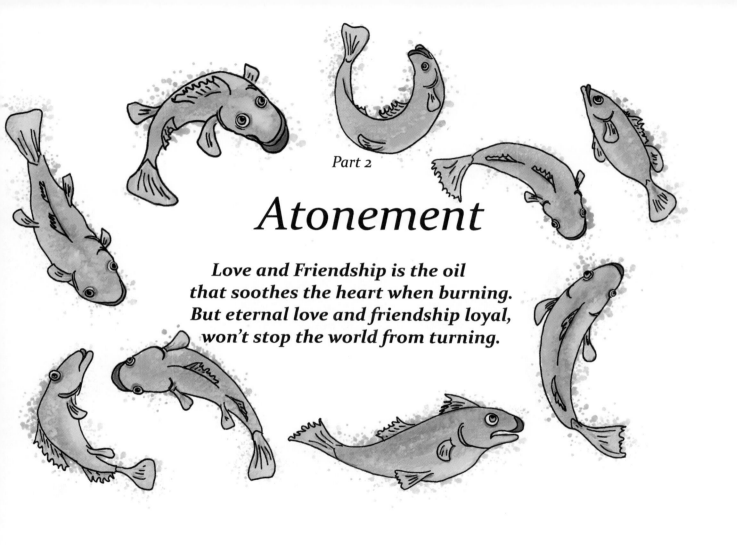

Part 2

Atonement

**Love and Friendship is the oil
that soothes the heart when burning.
But eternal love and friendship loyal,
won't stop the world from turning.**

Four and twenty years had passed
since the atrocity was viewed.
Now the wizard must confront
his past
to glean what had pursued.

He crawled up to the rocky mound,
hair white and face all wrinkly.
Though eyesight poor, he peered around
and saw it quite distinctly!

A camel's head, and fishy pans
sizzling on the rock beyond.
He blinked and took a second glance...

The camel's head was gone!

"After all these years,"
the wizard mused,
"how could this still be so?
Fishes so relentlessly perused
as they fry and burn below!

A camel has his camel ways
but none so cruel as these.
Never before has a mammal's gaze
brought marine life to its knees.

How far has this obsession reached?"
the purple wizard cried,
"This sick pursuit must be impeached
before more poor mites are fried!"

Now the wizard's mighty wand was raised.
His face was taut and fuming.
He faced the camel quite unfazed,
then these wise commands came booming...

"ALL CAMEL-KIND, I DO PROCLAIM
SHALL CEASE AQUATIC TORMENT,
AND PEACEFULLY GO FROM
WHENCE YOU CAME.
WHAT SAY YE TO MY COMMENT?"

The Camel he appeared content,
no emotion did he show.
Then half way up his eighth ascent,
he simply answered... "No!"

Taken aback by this curt reply,
the wizard watched aghast,
as again the camel jumped up high
to watch them breathe their last.

Then as dusk fell all around,
a storm brewed in the air.
The wizard dived for covered ground
among the trees and bushes there.

In the morning when the storm had passed
the wizard woke to an awesome sound.
He looked around to see at last
the camel sobbing on the ground.

Slowly forth the wizard shuffled
to view the sobbing camel.
He stood in silence weeps-a-muffled,
feeling compassion for the mammal.

Then he said unto the grizzling beast
"Why do you gurn and weep?
Perhaps your ethics changed at least,
while I slumbered in my sleep?"

The camel raised his reddened eyes,
tears flowed down his cheeks in flocks.
"No, No!" he blubbed
through sobbing sighs,
"I just stubbed my toe
on the rocks!"

"So you **do** feel pain!" the wizard cried
through this teary eyed commotion.
"I knew that somewhere deep inside
you harboured some emotion!"

"Yes, I have emotions too!"
the camel spat with fury!
"Of what concern is it to you?
Are you my judge and jury?"

"I merely meant that in some way
you've shown some indication,
that you keep emotions locked away
in some clandestine location!"

"So again I ask, why watch the fish,
their demise to run its course?
It seems to me still so fiendish,
where do you hide remorse?"

It was then the camel stopped his jump,
"I'll tell you where," he said.
"My remorse is stored inside my hump,
alongside my shame and dread".

For once the wizard had no voice,
such was his surprise!
Inside his hump he keeps by choice
that which would make him wise?

The camel said, "I'll tell you why
I store it all away!
So I can watch the fish head fry
while keeping shame at bay!"

"That's not the point", *the wizard yelled,*
"You can't hide away remorse!
For reason to be thus expelled
is against man's chosen course!"

"Who chose this course for man indeed?"
The camel clenched his fist.
"Name the one who first decreed
our pleasures we must resist?"

"It's not for us to question that"
the wizard said in reply,
"I could keep my shame inside my hat,
my conscience to deny!"

"To guide us through each passing day
and each tempestuous night,
the Gods have shown an easy way
to wrestle wrong from right".

"You're a righteous one," the camel screamed
"Have **YOU** felt no remorse?
Is your own salvation not redeemed
'til you change me from my course?"

"My sorrow may be in my hump
and my shame stored up for now,
but at least my fun's not in my rump
and some enjoyment I'll allow!"

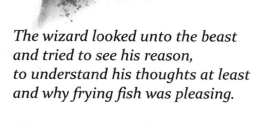

The wizard looked unto the beast
and tried to see his reason,
to understand his thoughts at least
and why frying fish was pleasing.

The wizard asked while open armed
"Why not release your feelings?
A life of peace with no fish harmed
is surely more appealing!"

The camel mused the wizard's words
on each and every jump,
then concluded that it **was** absurd
to secrete things in his hump.

The camel stopped and faced the sage
and said "I see your reasoning!
But **why** do I feel I must still engage
in watching fish fry with seasoning?"

"I don't **mean** to be so mean you see,
I just have to jump!
I hide away my misery
within my hairy hump".

The wizard mused a little more
then posed a searching question...
"If you feel your heart's a little sore
then here is my suggestion..."

"Open up the hump of truth!
Release all inside I say!
Release all unto the world forsooth!
Make this your judgement day!"

"Cast out your angst, your fear, your woe!
Your misery, sloth, and screams!
Your greed, your shame they all must go!
Replace with love and dreams!"

"And when your hump is free of hate
harbouring only love and wishes,
maybe then you'll liberate
those shoals of frying fishes?"

"If we can resolve this terrible past
and try to make amends,
then peace will be with us both at last
and always we'll be friends".

The camel clasped his hands in prayer!
He knelt then did decree,
"I've seen the light and do declare...
A new epiphany!"

With that the camel screwed his eyes
and bloated out his cheeks.
The wizard stood there mesmerised
through the camel's strains and shrieks.

The camel's hump glowed red and hot!
It trembled, throbbed and pulsed!
It steamed, it frothed, it smoked a lot!
The beast became convulsed!

With a dazzling, glaring flash of light
and a force that was volcanic,
the camel's hump lit up the night!
The wizard shook with panic.

And all those dark and wicked traits
were expelled in one eruption!
Out flew misery, sloth and hate,
greed, anger and corruption.

Arrogance flew out to the left,
pomposity to the right!
The hump dispersed until bereft
of all conceit and spite.

The wizard stood eyes tightly closed
as the fierce discharge subsided.
The camel rose, appeared composed
and to the wizard confided...

"From this day hence
my jumps will cease
and fish will fry no more,
for in my hump lies only peace,
with humility at its core".

With hand on heart the wizard cried
"The Gods will send their blessings,
for you **will** release the fishes fried
from their existence most distressing"

"Oh Bravo you! Oh bravo you!
My even-toed ungulate friend!
You've seen the light, your heart is true,
for that I must commend!"

The camel smiled and gave a nod
to the sage he once berated.
The camel's smile became quite broad
as the wiz reciprocated.

The wizard held the camel's toe,
he spoke in words sincere.
"You're cured my friend so I must go,
my work is finished here".

"Jump on my back the camel said,
and I will take you home.
To my own sanctuary you'll be led,
where you'll never be alone."

So the camel knelt upon the ground
and the wizard climbed the beast.
To the sanctuary they were bound
faraway in the East.

And as they journeyed on their trip
they pondered many things.
Like love and trust and friendship,
and what atonement brings.

Onward on their homeward quest
they crossed the dawn horizon,

then a distant figure heading west,
loomed as the sun was rising.

And soon the stranger came about
into the camel nation.
His fine apparel left no doubt
of his sorcery vocation.

With orange cloak and orange hat
and orange gloves and wand,
the youthful orange wizard sat
close to the rocks beyond.

He thought of great ambitions
though feet sore and body aching,
of magical new missions
and of dangerous undertakings.

But his thoughts hit an interruption
through an intermittent sound,
and the source of the disruption
was some jumping on the ground!

The youthful sage climbed up the rock
to view what was occurring.
He looked, he winced, he froze in shock
eyes wet and vision blurring.

An adolescent camel jumped
up to a sizzling dish!
The wizard shook, his heart it pumped
as he saw the frying fish!

Up and down the camel went
to watch the fishes fry,
but halfway down his fourth descent,
the wizard asked him, "Why...?"

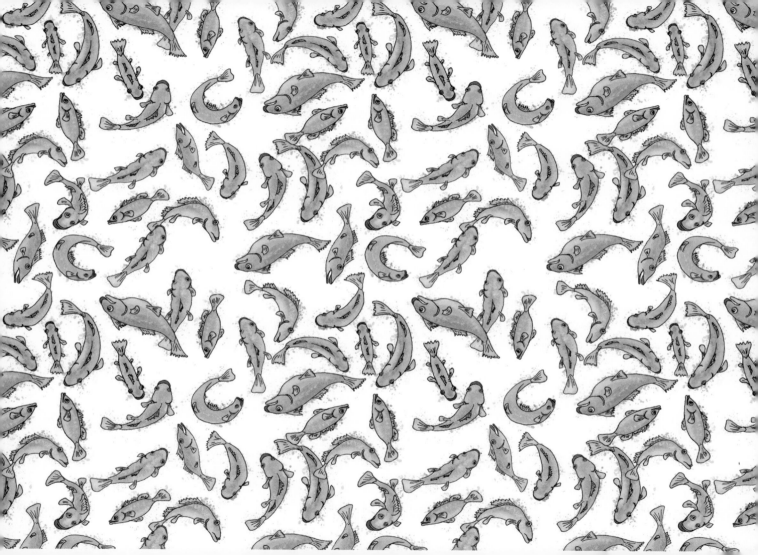

Printed in Great Britain
by Amazon

45138901R00032